AF228627

FACT AND FICTION OF THE WILD WEST

BY MARTHA LONDON

CONTENT CONSULTANT
Thomas Andrews, PhD
Professor of History
University of Colorado Boulder

Core Library

An Imprint of Abdo Publishing
abdobooks.com

Cover image: James "Wild Bill" Hickok was a famous lawman, showman, and gunfighter in the Wild West.

abdobooks.com

Published by Abdo Publishing, a division of ABDO, PO Box 398166, Minneapolis, Minnesota 55439. Copyright © 2022 by Abdo Consulting Group, Inc. International copyrights reserved in all countries. No part of this book may be reproduced in any form without written permission from the publisher. Core Library™ is a trademark and logo of Abdo Publishing.

Printed in the United States of America, North Mankato, Minnesota
052021
092021

Cover Photo: Photo12/Universal Images Group/Getty Images
Interior Photos: Matt York/AP/Shutterstock Images, 4–5; Red Line Editorial, 7, 17; JT Vintage/Glasshouse Images/Alamy, 12–13; Everett Collection/Shutterstock Images, 20, 29, 37; T. W. Smillie/Wikimedia Commons, 22; Zuri Swimmer/Alamy, 24–25, 43; Victorian Traditions/Shutterstock Images, 32–33, 45; Underwood Archives/Archive Photos/Getty Images, 34

Editor: Aubrey Zalewski
Series Designer: Ryan Gale

Library of Congress Control Number: 2020948288

Publisher's Cataloging-in-Publication Data

Names: London, Martha, author.
Title: Fact and fiction of the wild west / by Martha London
Description: Minneapolis, Minnesota : Abdo Publishing, 2022 | Series: Fact and fiction of American history | Includes online resources and index.
Identifiers: ISBN 9781532195136 (lib. bdg.) | ISBN 9781098215446 (ebook)
Subjects: LCSH: Frontier and pioneer life--United States--Juvenile literature. | West (U.S.)--Juvenile literature. | Truthfulness and falsehood--Juvenile literature. | Public opinion--Juvenile literature.
Classification: DDC 978--dc23

CONTENTS

O.K.
CORRAL
GUNFIGHT SITE
ENTER HERE
O.K. CORRAL
GUNFIGHT SITE
WALK WHERE THEY

GUNFIGHT AT THE O.K. CORRAL

In 1881, one of the most famous shootouts in history occurred in Tombstone, Arizona. Virgil Earp was the town marshal. He recruited his brothers Wyatt and Morgan as deputies. They fought outlaws in Tombstone. Their friend Doc Holliday joined them in the shootout. On the other side were the McLaury and Clanton brothers. These brothers were part of an outlaw gang called the Cowboys.

The Earps had made many claims against the Cowboys. Among them was

Tombstone, Arizona, made the O.K. Corral gunfight site a tourist attraction.

that the Cowboys were illegally armed. Only sheriffs and marshals could have weapons in Tombstone. On October 26, 1881, the Earps and Doc Holliday faced the Cowboys outside the O.K. Corral. There were likely at least eight men in the standoff.

The lawmen warned the Cowboys to put down their weapons. They refused. A gunfight erupted. In less than a minute, three men from the gang were dead. Holliday and two of the Earp brothers were wounded. But they had protected the 7,000 people of Tombstone from outlaws.

This is how the story of the O.K. Corral is often told. But the

MANIFEST DESTINY

John O'Sullivan coined the term "Manifest Destiny" in an 1845 magazine article. Manifest Destiny was a somewhat widely held belief that the United States was destined to expand west across the continent. This belief was used to justify obtaining more land and relocating Native American tribes.

UNITED STATES
EXPANSION

Before Europeans arrived in North America, Native Americans lived there. Over time, the European countries claimed the native peoples' land. The United States eventually took control of the land through wars, treaties, and purchases. The map below shows the United States' expansion. Why do you think the United States wanted this land? How does the map help you understand the events of westward expansion?

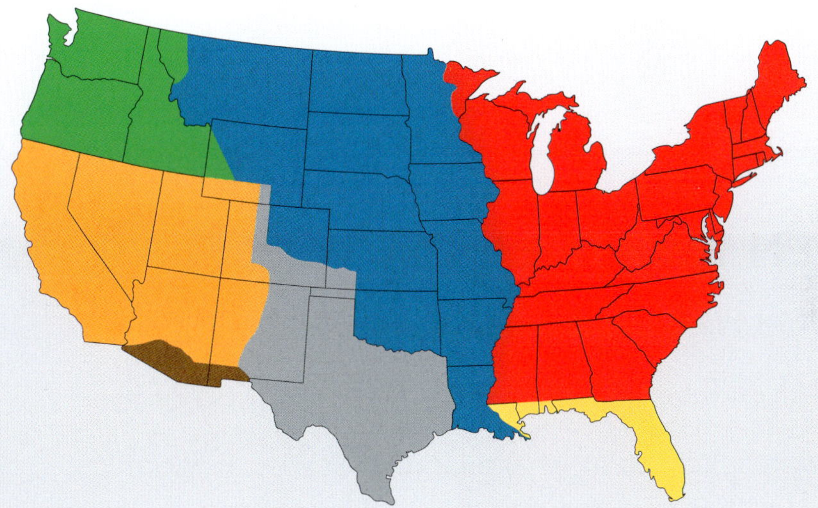

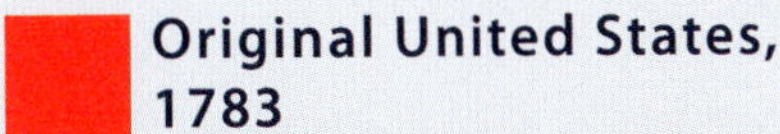
Original United States, 1783

Louisiana Purchase from France, 1803

Purchase of Florida from Spain, 1819

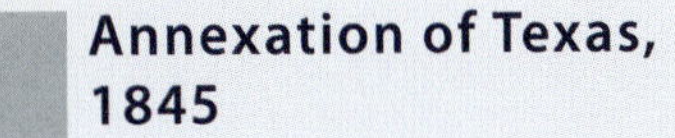
Annexation of Texas, 1845

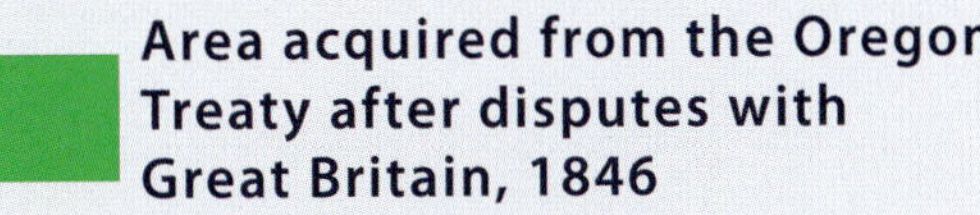
Area acquired from the Oregon Treaty after disputes with Great Britain, 1846

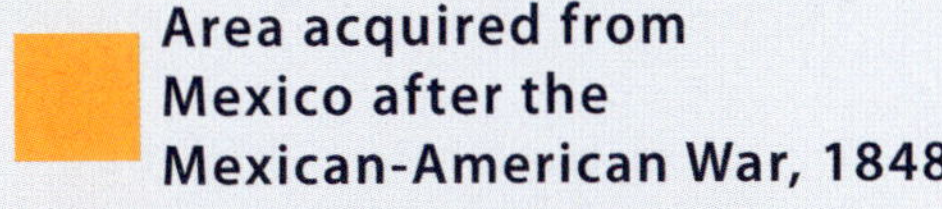
Area acquired from Mexico after the Mexican-American War, 1848

Gadsden Purchase from Mexico, 1853

truth is not so clear. The Earps may not have been the heroes people thought they were. The Earps and the Cowboys were rivals. The McLaury and Clanton brothers claimed the Earps targeted them unfairly. They said that the Earps acted for themselves and not for the law. They felt that the Earps had used their own anger against the McLaurys and Clantons to justify the shootout. The Earps had also been accused of robbing stagecoaches and committing other crimes. As with many famous tales from the Wild West, it can be hard to separate fact from fiction.

WHEN WAS THE WEST WILD?

The Wild West was a cultural area west of the Mississippi River. It existed during the period of the westward expansion of the United States. People had settled westward since the 1700s. But Western settlements boomed in the 1800s. In 1803, President Thomas Jefferson bought French territory west of the Mississippi River. This was called the Louisiana Purchase. It doubled the size of the United States. Over the next

90 years, millions of settlers relocated westward. They made their homes across most of the United States.

Some of those going west were looking for riches. Prospectors searched for land that held gold or silver. Miners collected the precious metals. Their families came with them. Others went west because of the Homestead Act. The US Congress passed this act in 1862. The act gave US citizens 160 acres (65 ha) of land for a small fee. Settlers needed to build a home

HEINMOT TOOYALAKEKT

Heinmot Tooyalakekt was a Nez Perce leader. US government leaders knew him as Chief Joseph. He worked tirelessly to avoid conflict with the US government. However, the Nez Perce were consistently pushed out of their lands in Idaho and Oregon when prospectors found gold. Frustrated, Heinmot Tooyalakekt met with Congress in 1879. In his speech he said, "Good words will not give my people a home where they can live in peace and take care of themselves. I am tired of talk that comes to nothing."

and farm the land. While many settlers were able to build a new life out West, approximately half of the homesteaders failed.

Westward expansion brought conflict between the settlers and the Native American nations who already lived on the land. They had been there for thousands of years. Many settlers allowed cattle to graze illegally on Native American lands. Mining booms pushed Native peoples from their homes. As settlers moved westward, Native American groups were often pushed out.

Today, movies, books, and television shows paint a romantic picture of the Wild West. Stories often glorify cowboys and sheriffs. They show Native American stereotypes. Many stories exaggerate events to make them seem more exciting. The term *Wild West* itself supports the myth of an untamed land. The facts of the Wild West are very different from the fiction people see portrayed today.

STRAIGHT TO THE
SOURCE

Paul Hedren is a historian and author. He wrote a book about the Wild West. In an interview, he discussed researching his book:

I grew up celebrating things like the construction of the transcontinental railroads and the "beef bonanza" and see them still as extraordinary national accomplishments that truly helped define America. But this book forced me to see it all in quite a different light. The Indian barrier had to be removed before the Northern Pacific [Railway] could advance westward from Bismarck. The northern buffalo herd had to be eliminated before cattle could spread across the same range. And the plight of the Sioux and Northern Cheyennes in the early reservation era is a pretty tough story. . . . There are pretty dramatic human and environmental consequences lurking in this great drama.

Source: Johnny D. Boggs. "Interview with Historian Paul Hedren." *HistoryNet*, n.d., historynet.com. Accessed 25 Aug. 2020.

CONSIDER YOUR AUDIENCE

Adapt this passage for a different audience, such as your principal or friends. Write a blog post conveying this same information for the new audience. How does your post differ from the original text and why?

CULTURE CLASH

In the West, conflicts between white Americans and Native American communities were common. Many white people believed Native Americans were not equal to white people. Newspaper articles and theater shows depicted Native Americans as violent or uncivilized.

One of the shows that did this was Buffalo Bill's Wild West show. It ran from 1883 to 1916. Performers toured throughout the United States and Europe. The Wild West show had Native American performers. There were reenactments of historical events such as

William Frederick Cody, also known as Buffalo Bill, started Buffalo Bill's Wild West show.

the Pony Express and the Battle of the Little Bighorn. The show was theatrical and meant to entertain. The "cowboys and Indians" were stereotypes. It showed cowboys as heroes and Native Americans as villains.

CONFLICT WITH SETTLERS

Many narratives presented Native American communities as violent. People spread stories of Native Americans attacking wagon trains. But the reality of settlers moving westward was much different.

Settlers had many peaceful interactions with Native communities. Few tribes wanted conflict with white settlers. Communities traded with settlers. They helped settlers find trails. But peace didn't last. Settlers forced tribes from their lands. They stole resources. They killed Native Americans. As a result, some Native Americans attacked settlers to protect their families and land.

STEALING LAND

The US government valued the land Native Americans lived on. Officials used treaties to take what they wanted for US citizens and businesses. In some treaties, the United States purchased Native homelands. In exchange, the US government promised lands for Native communities west of the Mississippi River. However, other Native nations often already lived in these areas. This caused more conflict. In some cases, groups such as the Ojibwe (Anishinaabe) in Minnesota sold portions of their lands. They were allowed to continue hunting and gathering on the lands. However, they often ran into obstacles when trying to continue using the lands.

Other groups were forced out. In 1835, members of the Cherokee Nation signed a treaty with the United States. Many people of the nation refused to acknowledge it. The US military forced those who refused to leave from their land. This removal was part of what became known as the Trail of Tears.

During the Trail of Tears, US government officers forced Native peoples from their homes in Tennessee, Alabama, Mississippi, Florida, and Georgia. Between 1838 and 1839, the US government led them to current-day Oklahoma. They were forced to leave without enough supplies. On the trail, the people suffered from disease, exhaustion, and poor nutrition. Additionally, they were not given enough money to reestablish their communities once they arrived in Oklahoma. Historians estimate 15,000 Cherokee, Chickasaw, Choctaw, Seminole, and Muscogee people died on the trail.

In 1868, the US government and the Western Sioux signed a treaty. This treaty reserved the Dakota Territory

LAND
SEIZURE

The United States seized Native American lands using treaties and executive orders. Executive orders are made by the president to manage the federal government. Between 1776 and 1887, the United States took approximately 1.5 billion acres (0.6 billion ha) from Native American peoples. The chart below shows how much land was taken each decade. What do you notice about the chart? How does seeing the chart help you understand the amount of land that was taken from Native American peoples?

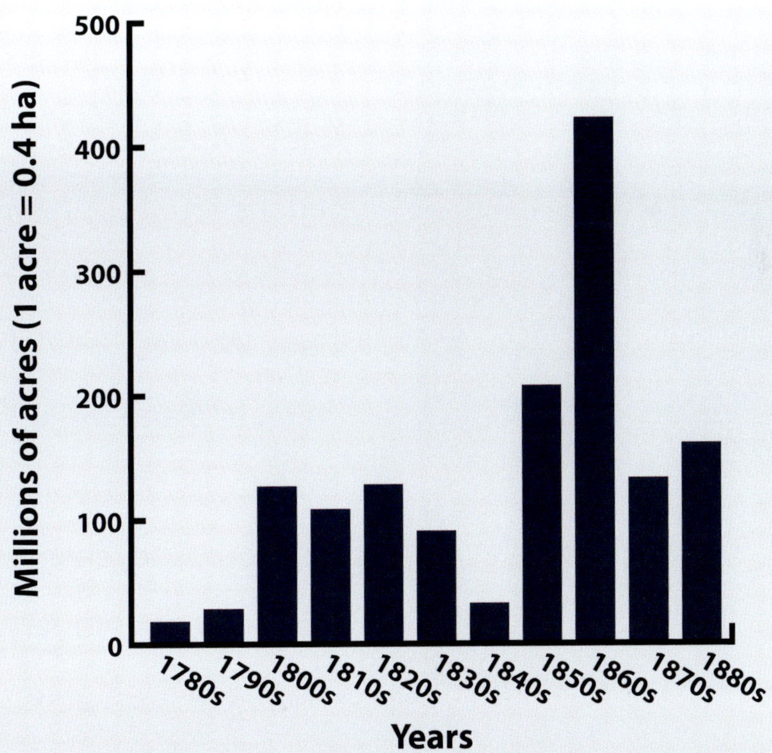

Source: "The Invasion of America." *eHistory.org*, youtube.com, 2 June 2014. Accessed 26 Aug. 2020.

west of the Missouri River for the Western Sioux. This area was a small portion of their ancestral homelands. During the Black Hills gold rush in the 1870s, the US government illegally redrew the boundaries of the lands. It took more of the lands that belonged to Native communities.

AT WAR

The US Army and Native American nations fought in many conflicts. The Great Sioux War was one of them. It lasted from 1876 to 1877. The Northern Cheyenne and Northern Arapaho Tribes allied with the Great Sioux Nation.

One of the most famous battles was the Battle of the Greasy Grass in current-day Montana. The battle was also known as the Battle of the Little Bighorn.

Sitting Bull (Tatanka-Iyotanka) was a Lakota Sioux leader. The Lakota people are part of the Great Sioux Nation. Sitting Bull wanted to protect the nation's lands from the US government. On June 25, 1876, General George Custer of the US Army came upon a group of Sioux and Cheyenne warriors. Sitting Bull was one of their main leaders. Approximately 650 US soldiers met 2,000 Sioux and Cheyenne warriors near the Greasy Grass River. Greater numbers, better weapons, and stronger tactics meant the warriors easily defeated the army. Two-hundred and sixty-eight US soldiers died during the battle. Reports say Sitting Bull lost 50 warriors.

Sioux and Cheyenne leaders hoped the victory at the Greasy Grass would cause the US government to leave Native American lands alone. However, that

was not the case. In 1876 and 1877, the US Army and the Sioux, Northern Arapaho, and Northern Cheyenne peoples engaged in a series of battles and negotiations.

THE GHOST DANCE MOVEMENT

In 1889, a religious movement called the Ghost Dance began. A man named Wovoka was part of the Walker River Paiute Tribe. He said that doing the rituals of the Ghost Dance would restore Native lands and bring peace. The rituals included a ceremonial dance and songs. Many Native Americans took part in the Ghost Dance movement. The movement was mostly peaceful. But some Sioux used it to encourage violence against white people who oppressed them. White officials were afraid Ghost Dancers would rise up against settlers. Officials told the military to relocate or arrest leaders of the Ghost Dance movement.

In December 1890, Chief Spotted Elk (Si Tanka) was leading a group of approximately 350 Minneconjou

Sitting Bull (Tatanka-Iyotanka) became the principal chief of the Great Sioux Nation in 1867.

Chief Spotted Elk (Si Tanka) became chief of the Minneconjou in 1874.

Lakota people. Many were part of the Ghost Dance movement. They were on their way to a Lakota stronghold near Pine Ridge, South Dakota, for safety. Then US troops surrounded them near Wounded Knee Creek. Spotted Elk wanted to avoid bloodshed. He promised to surrender peacefully.

The US troops ordered the Minneconjou to hand over all weapons. A soldier tried to wrestle a gun away from one man. The gun went off. US troops opened fire. The Minneconjou tried to run away. But the soldiers chased and shot them. They killed as many as 300 Minneconjou people. Initially, the government said the event at Wounded Knee was a battle. They claimed the Minneconjou were hostile. They said soldiers were defending themselves. But accounts from survivors and other witnesses proved it was a massacre.

EXPLORE ONLINE

Chapter Two discusses the displacement of Native Americans throughout the American West. The website below gives more information about Sitting Bull (Tatanka-Iyotanka). As you know, every source is different. How is the information from the website the same as the information in Chapter Two? What new information did you learn from the website?

SITTING BULL: SPIRITUAL LEADER AND MILITARY LEADER

abdocorelibrary.com/fact-fiction-wild-west

SHARPSHOOTERS AND OUTLAWS

The Wild West may be best known for sharpshooters and outlaws. Some famous sharpshooters worked for the law. Others worked against the law. Some did both at different points in their lives. No matter what role sharpshooters played, stories about them were often much more glamorous than the truth.

JOAQUÍN MURRIETA

The California Gold Rush brought people from all backgrounds to the the state, including some from other countries. Competition grew and miners of all backgrounds who once

Joaquín Murrieta's legend was first recorded in a novel by John Rollin Ridge (Yellow Bird).

worked side-by-side became increasingly prejudiced toward one another. Yankees, or people from the United States, wanted to keep foreign miners out of the gold mines. California officials passed laws. One law taxed foreign-born miners. Another controlled where Mexican Americans were allowed to travel. These laws angered Mexican Americans.

One story goes that Joaquín Murrieta, a Mexican American, wanted to get back at the Yankees. He led groups of outlaws. They robbed gold miners. They held up stagecoaches. The legend says that the California governor offered a reward for Murrieta, dead or alive. Over the years, writers built up Murrieta's myth.

WILD BILL

James "Wild Bill" Hickok is often remembered as a hero of the Wild West. He was featured in novels and westerns. Hickok served in the US Army during the Civil War (1861–1865). Later, he became a lawman. He was known as one of the best shooters in the West.

One of his most famous legends was the gunfight at Rock Creek in 1861. The most common story says Hickok was riding with a group of US soldiers in Nebraska. He stopped to visit his friend Jane Wellman and her husband, Horace. Jane told Hickok that a gang led by David McCanles was coming to get him. When McCanles arrived, Hickok acted quickly. He shot McCanles and five gang members. He knocked out one more and then beat three in hand-to-hand combat. Hickok single-handedly defeated an entire group of armed men.

The story was published for the first time six years later in *Harper's* magazine.

ANNIE OAKLEY

Buffalo Bill's Wild West show had many sharpshooters. Audiences assumed these shooters came from the Wild West. But in reality, performers came from all over the United States. Annie Oakley was one of these performers. Oakley grew up in Ohio, far from the rough-and-tumble Wild West. But her skills as a sharpshooter impressed every person she came in contact with. She was able to shoot dimes out of the air and split a playing card on its edge.

Historians generally agree that the published story was not completely true. The Wellmans most likely aided Hickok. Additionally, the gang was just David McCanles, his son Monroe, and two other men. They were coming to collect money that Horace owed them. Monroe claimed they were unarmed. It is likely that Hickok or Horace Wellman attacked first and the men tried to run away.

CALAMITY JANE

Martha Jane Burke was better known as Calamity Jane. There are many stories of Calamity Jane as a gunslinging cowgirl. They often say she wore men's clothing, drank alcohol, and swore like a man. Some of these things were true. But many facts of Burke's life were exaggerated over time, even by Burke herself.

Part of Calamity Jane's legend came from her association with Wild Bill Hickok. Some stories say they were friends. Burke even claimed they were married.

However, most historians believe it is unlikely that she knew Hickok well.

Burke probably wore dresses most of the time. Photographs exist of her in pants. However, historians believe these photos were most likely for shows that she participated in. She sometimes worked jobs that were common for a woman in the 1800s. Burke was a laundress. She also worked as a dancer in saloons. Saloons were bars that sold food and alcohol.

They often had music and dancing as entertainment. She also tried her hand at ranching. Between 1895 and 1901, Burke performed in Wild West shows in the Midwest.

BILLY THE KID

William H. Bonney Jr. was still young when he became Billy the Kid. In his early teens, Bonney began stealing. He became an infamous gunslinger. He joined gangs that traveled across the southwest United States and into Mexico. A sharpshooting criminal, the Kid is believed to have shot 27 people.

Billy the Kid was arrested at 21 by Sheriff Pat Garrett. The Kid was sentenced to hang for his crimes. But he escaped. He shot two deputies. Billy the Kid was on the run. Garrett eventually caught up with him and shot him.

The stories of Billy the Kid live on. Two people claimed to have been the real Kid. Both men said the sheriff shot the wrong man in 1881. One story even says Garrett helped the Kid escape into Texas. Historians doubt these claims.

FURTHER EVIDENCE

Chapter Three covers some of the most famous gunslingers of the Wild West. What was one of the main points of this chapter? What evidence is included to support this point? Read the article at the website below. Does the information on the website support the main point of the chapter? Does it present new evidence?

WHO WAS BILLY THE KID?

abdocorelibrary.com/fact-fiction-wild-west

LOOKING TO PROSPER

Many people who went to the West were looking for new opportunities. Some searched for land. Others looked for riches. White people moving to the West saw it as a vast and empty area. They could make a new life on the frontier. However, Native American peoples had been living there for thousands of years.

ALREADY OCCUPIED

The West was not empty. Hundreds of thousands of Native Americans lived there. Before the California Gold Rush began in 1848, approximately 200,000 Native people lived

Settlers moved West with their families in wagons.

During the California Gold Rush, miners tried to push the Hoopa Valley Tribe out of their lands in Northern California.

in California. They formed more than 500 tribal groups. The local communities included the Paiute Tribe, the Miwok people, and others. Each tribe had several smaller bands.

Miners and settlers moved into the territories, pushing Native peoples from their homelands. The settlers took over lands that were sacred to the Native peoples and killed or caused the death of many Native Americans. By 1870, there were only

12,000 Native people in California.

Settlers harmed Native American communities in many ways. For example, they used up resources. Plains nations such as the Sioux relied on bison herds. But settlers killed the animals for sport and for hides. Settlers also enslaved Native Americans. State and local governments made it legal for white settlers to take Native children away from their families. Because of other laws, Native communities could not sue white settlers. Newspapers told untrue stories about Native communities, including stories about attacks on white people. This supported racist beliefs that many white Americans held.

THE GOLDEN LAND

Precious metals such as gold and silver existed across the western US territories. When someone found a deposit, thousands of people flocked to the location. Miners would stake claims to the land. This meant that they had permission to mine the land. In 1848, people found huge gold deposits in California. This was the start of the California Gold Rush.

Between 1848 and 1855, approximately 300,000 settlers arrived in California, pushing out or killing Native American residents. Many people today believe the California settlers were all from the United States. But news of the gold traveled around the world. Miners from South America, China, Australia, Mexico, and Europe also arrived.

Within a year of the discovery of gold in California, approximately 80,000 miners arrived from around the world.

Despite the large deposits, few prospectors struck it rich. Many of the claims had barely enough gold to cover the cost of their labor. Additionally, conditions in mining towns could be harsh, with few streets, buildings, or wells. Miners worked from dawn until dusk. And most towns did not have doctors to treat illness or injury.

But not all boomtowns were rough. Boomtowns in areas with rich silver or gold deposits thrived.

This was the case in Tombstone, Arizona. A prospector discovered silver in the area in 1877. Like California's gold rush, silver brought thousands of people to Tombstone.

The town was wealthy. As settlers from the eastern United States arrived, so did more conveniences. Throughout the 1880s, the town had many shops. There was running water in homes and businesses. There was even an ice-skating rink in the desert town. The settlers had gone West to create a similar life to what they had back East. But boomtowns did not last forever. For example, Tombstone faced

MINING ACCIDENTS

For thousands of people, mining in the West was an opportunity for a new start. But mining came with serious hazards. Miners faced dirty and dangerous conditions. Accidents were common. People lost fingers or eyes. Cave-ins, explosions, and fires killed many miners. Additionally, miners breathed in dust and other tiny particles. This led to an increased risk of lung diseases.

flooded mines, low silver prices, and labor problems. By 1900, the population went from the thousands to less than 700.

FINDING LAND TO CALL HOME

In addition to mining, farming was another important part of the West. Most settlers moved westward in search of land that was cheap or free. Cities were expensive and dirty. But the West was seen as a paradise for farming. With so much open space, people thought it would be easy to grow crops.

But farming was far from glamorous. Some boomtowns grew because of the farming industry. But many homesteads were miles from town. Settlers could become lonely. Additionally, wildfires, pests, and drought made growing crops difficult or impossible.

Raising cattle was not any easier. A few ranches were able to raise thousands of cattle. But then cowboys had to drive the cattle from the prairie to the railroads and then to market. Moving that many animals was difficult. Cattle wandered away. Cowboys had to constantly be aware of animals that fell behind.

Cowboys also worked under terrible conditions. In movies, cowboys are free to do whatever they want. They are gunfighters who save the day and ride off into the sunset. But the reality was far from Hollywood's shine. Cowboys were often underpaid. They worked long hours under the hot sun. Cowboys in the movies are often white men. But in reality, many cowboys were of African American, Mexican American, or Native American descent.

The Wild West was a time of discoveries and expansion. But stories of the Wild West may ignore or justify the mistreatment of certain groups of people. Disagreements over Wild West-era treaties between the US government and Native American nations continue to this day. The stories also glorify gunslingers and lawmen. The West could be exciting. But it was also a rough and lawless place.

STRAIGHT TO THE
SOURCE

Louise Clappe lived in California in the mid-1800s. She followed her husband to a gold mining town called Rich Bar in 1851. Clappe wrote letters to her sister in Massachusetts. Clappe talked about people's reaction to her decision to move to Rich Bar:

Some said that I ought to be put into a strait-jacket, for I was undoubtedly mad to think of such a thing. Some said that I should never get there alive, and if I did, would not stay a month. . . . One lady declared, in a burst of outraged modesty, that it was absolutely indelicate to think of living in such a large population of men, where, at the most, there were but two or three women. I laughed merrily at their mournful [predictions], and started [happily] for Marysville, where I arrived in a couple of days, ready to commence my journey to Rich Bar.

Source: Louise Clappe. *The Shirley Letters from California Mines*. Thomas C. Russell, editor, 1922, tile.loc.gov. Accessed 25 Aug. 2020.

WHAT'S THE BIG IDEA?

Take a close look at this passage. What is the main connection being made between women and the gold rush? What can you tell about how people saw boomtowns and their safety? How does Clappe's response support or go against those views?

IMPORTANT DATES

10,000 BCE

Native Americans have settlements across North America.

1803

President Thomas Jefferson makes the Louisiana Purchase. This doubles the size of the United States and begins an era of increased settlement in the West.

1838

The Trail of Tears, one of many instances in which the US government pushed Native Americans out of their homelands, begins. Thousands of Native American people are forced to relocate to Oklahoma.

1848

Gold is discovered in California. This prompts approximately 300,000 people to flock to the state. Many of the 200,000 Native Americans who live in California are displaced, are killed, or die of disease.

1862

Congress passes the Homestead Act, which gives 160 acres (65 ha) to people looking to settle on the frontier.

1876

Lakota Sioux and Cheyenne warriors defeat US soldiers at the Battle of the Greasy Grass. This is one of many conflicts between Native American peoples and the US Army.

1881

On October 26, the shootout at the O.K. Corral occurs in Tombstone, Arizona.

1890

US soldiers kill approximately 350 Minneconjou Lakota people near Wounded Knee Creek. Some people claim it was a battle, but it was actually a massacre.

STOP AND ★THINK

Tell the Tale

Chapter Four of this book discusses boomtowns in the West. Imagine you are in a Wild West boomtown. Write 200 words about the people and things you see in the town. Why are you there and what are you doing?

Surprise Me

Chapter One discusses what the Wild West was. After reading this book, what two or three facts about the Wild West did you find most surprising? Write a few sentences about each fact. Why did you find each fact surprising?

Dig Deeper

After reading this book, what questions do you still have about the Wild West? With an adult's help, find a few reliable sources that can help you answer your questions. Write a paragraph about what you learned.

Why Do I Care?

You weren't alive during the Wild West, but that doesn't mean you can't learn about how American settlers and government leaders treated Native Americans. How has that treatment affected those communities today? How would you feel if you were forced to move from your home?

GLOSSARY

annexation
the act of adding an area of land to a country or state

exaggerate
to make something seem more exciting or impressive

homestead
an area of US public land that people could live on if they filed paperwork and promised to develop it

infamous
known for a negative reason

massacre
the act of killing a group of people who are helpless or not resisting

reenactment
a performance that retells what happened during an event, such as a battle

ritual
a ceremonial act, such as a song or dance

stagecoach
a horse-drawn carriage that carries mail and passengers on a regular route and schedule

stereotype
an overly simple view of a person or group of people

treaty
a formal agreement between two authorities, such as states or nations

ONLINE RESOURCES

To learn more about facts and fiction of the Wild West, visit our free resource websites below.

Visit **abdocorelibrary.com** or scan this QR code for free Common Core resources for teachers and students, including vetted activities, multimedia, and booklinks, for deeper subject comprehension.

Visit **abdobooklinks.com** or scan this QR code for free additional online weblinks for further learning. These links are routinely monitored and updated to provide the most current information available.

LEARN MORE

Powell, Marie. *Traditional Stories of the Plains Nations*. Abdo Publishing, 2018.

Yasuda, Anita. *Women of the American West*. Abdo Publishing, 2017.

INDEX

About the Author

Martha London is a writer and educator. She lives in Minnesota. When she isn't writing, you can find her in the woods on the back of a horse.